THE CHINESE MIRROR

SAN DIEGO NEW YORK LONDON

VOYAGER BOOKS
HARCOURT
BRACE &
COMPANY

PRINTED IN HONG KONG

THE CHINESE MIRROR

ADAPTED FROM
A KOREAN FOLKTALE BY
MIRRA
GINSBURG
ILLUSTRATED BY
MARGOT
ZEMACH

The Library of Congress has cataloged the hardcover
edition as follows:
Ginsburg, Mirra.
The Chinese mirror.
Summary: A retelling of a traditional Korean tale
in which a mirror brought from China causes confusion
within a family as each member looks in it and sees a
different stranger.
[Folklore—Korea.] I. Zemach, Margot, ill.
II. Title.
PZ6.1.G455Ch 1987 398.2'7'09519 (R) 86-22940
ISBN 0-15-200420-3
ISBN 0-15-217508-3 pb

M L K J

TO GRETA, MAYA, AND MARK

— M.G.

FOR ODETTE

— M.Z.

There was a time, long, long ago, when no one in our village had ever seen a mirror. One day a villager went on a distant journey, all the way to China.

There, he went into a store and saw a strange round shiny thing. He looked at it, and a man's face looked back at him. He smiled, and the man smiled back at him. He stuck out his tongue, and the man stuck out his tongue. "Sell it to me," he said to the storekeeper. And he brought the mirror home with him.

At home he hid the mirror in a trunk, afraid its magic might be lost if everybody saw it. Once in a while he'd take it out secretly, laugh with pleasure, and then hide it again.

"Why is he laughing when there is nothing to laugh at?" his wife wondered, and began to watch him. One morning she saw him take a small round shiny thing out of the trunk, look into it, and smile. When he went out, she took the mirror and glanced into it.

"Oh, oh!" she cried. "The cruel, faithless man!" And she ran to her mother-in-law, wailing, "My faithless husband, your son, brought home a pretty, young wife from China, and keeps her hidden in the trunk. Look at her, there she is!"

"Stop wailing," said her mother-in-law, "and let me see the young beauty."

She glanced into the mirror, and burst out laughing. "My son may not be very clever," she said. "But why would he bring home a wrinkled old crone? No, there must be something else to it. He'd never get himself such a wife, it's just your foolish jealousy."

At that moment the man's father walked in and wondered why his daughter-in-law was crying and his wife laughing.

"Let me see for myself," he said.

He looked, and shrugged his shoulders, and said, "You sillies. This is not a woman, either young or old. It is our neighbor's grandpa, with his bald head and gray beard."

They kept looking and looking. But the young wife kept seeing a pretty young woman. The old woman kept seeing a wrinkled old crone. The old man kept seeing the neighbor's grandpa.

And none could convince the others that they were wrong.

They put the mirror back in the trunk, still arguing.

Now, the man and his wife had a little son.

"What are they arguing about?"

he asked himself. "Let me see."

When they were all gone, he took the mirror and looked in, and saw a boy with a nice round pebble in his hand.

"Oh, oh!" he yelled. "The nasty brat stole my pebble!"

A neighbor happened to be passing by.

"Why are you crying?" he asked. "Who stole your pebble?"

The boy held out the mirror and the man looked into it.

"You big fat bully," he shouted. "How dare you hurt little children?"

He banged his fist into the bully's face. Out flew the mirror, crashed against the wall, and scattered into a hundred shiny splinters.

And that was the end of the stranger who looked at the traveler, the young beauty from China, the wrinkled old crone, the neighbor's grandpa, the nasty brat who stole pebbles, and the big fat bully who hurt little boys.

The illustrations in this book were inspired
by the paintings of two eighteenth-century
Korean genre painters,
Sin Yun-bok and Kim Hong-do.

The illustrations in this book were done in watercolor on Crescent illustration board.
The text type was set in ITC Usherwood Book.
The display type was set via photo typositor in Auriol Bold.
Composition by Thompson Type, San Diego, California
Color separations by Heinz Weber Inc., Los Angeles, California
Printed by South China Printing Co. Ltd., Hong Kong
Production supervision by Warren Wallerstein and Ginger Boyer
Designed by Joy Chu